The Flying Garbanzos

by Barney
Saltzberg

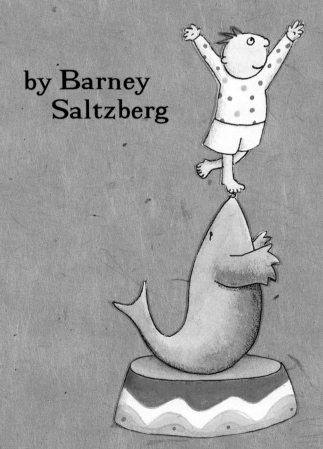

Dragonfly Books®

Crown Publishers • New York

DRAGONFLY BOOKS® PUBLISHED BY CROWN PUBLISHERS

Copyright © 1998 by Barney Saltzberg

Published by Crown Publishers, a division of Random House, Inc.,
201 East 50th Street, New York, New York 10022

www.randomhouse.com/kids

Library of Congress Cataloging-in-Publication Data
Barney Saltzberg.
The Flying Garbanzos / by Barney Saltzberg.
p.   cm.
Summary: The World-Famous Flying Garbanzos try to keep up with Beanie and his
flyaway cake on his second birthday.
[1. Birthdays—Fiction. 2. Birthday cakes—Fiction. 3. Acrobats—Fiction.]
I. Title.   PZ7.S1552Fl   1998   [E]—dc21   97-45575

ISBN   0-517-70978-3 (trade)
0-517-70979-1 (lib. bdg.)
0-517-88599-9 (pbk.)

First Dragonfly Books® edition: June 2000

Printed in the United States of America
10 9 8 7 6 5 4 3 2 1

For Andrea Cascardi,
editor "extraordinaire," who has
continually encouraged me
to take risks and dance across
the high wire!

It was a special day at the house of
the World-Famous Flying Garbanzos.

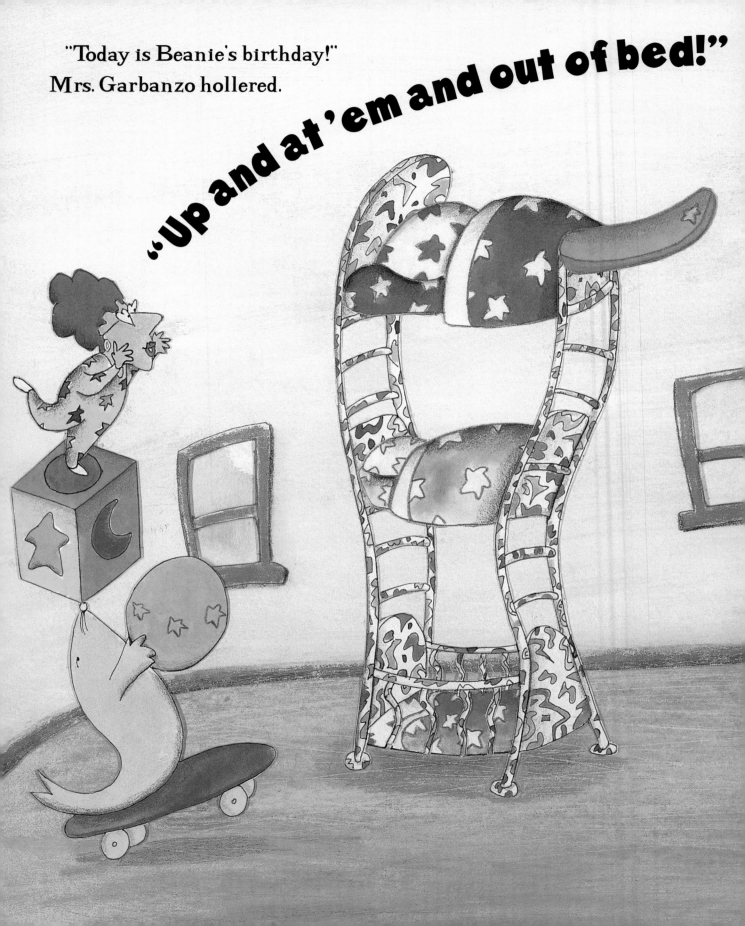

"Today is Beanie's birthday!"
Mrs. Garbanzo hollered.

"Up and at 'em and out of bed!"

Ima and Jake flipped and flew,
singing over and over.
"Yahoo—Beanie's two!
Yahoo, yahoo, yahoo!"

Beanie was already up and swinging
in the kitchen with Harry the monkey.
"Happy birthday, Beanie!"
said Mrs. Garbanzo.

"Birthday!"

shouted Beanie.

"My birthday!"

"Yes!" said Mrs. Garbanzo. "And we're
having your party this afternoon!"
"Cake!" squealed Beanie.
"Are you going to sing to your cake?"
asked Mrs. Garbanzo.
"No!" laughed Beanie.
Mrs. Garbanzo laughed, too.

Mr. Garbanzo was out
walking the poodles.

Mrs. Garbanzo said,
"Come in for pancakes!"

"Birthday cakes!"
said Beanie.

"*Pancakes!*"
said Mr. Garbanzo.

"Oh!" said Beanie.

At breakfast, Ima complained.
"Jake's juggling at the table again!"
"Your brother's *always* throwing something up in the air!" said Mrs. Garbanzo. "Now make room for Beanie's birthday breakfast!"

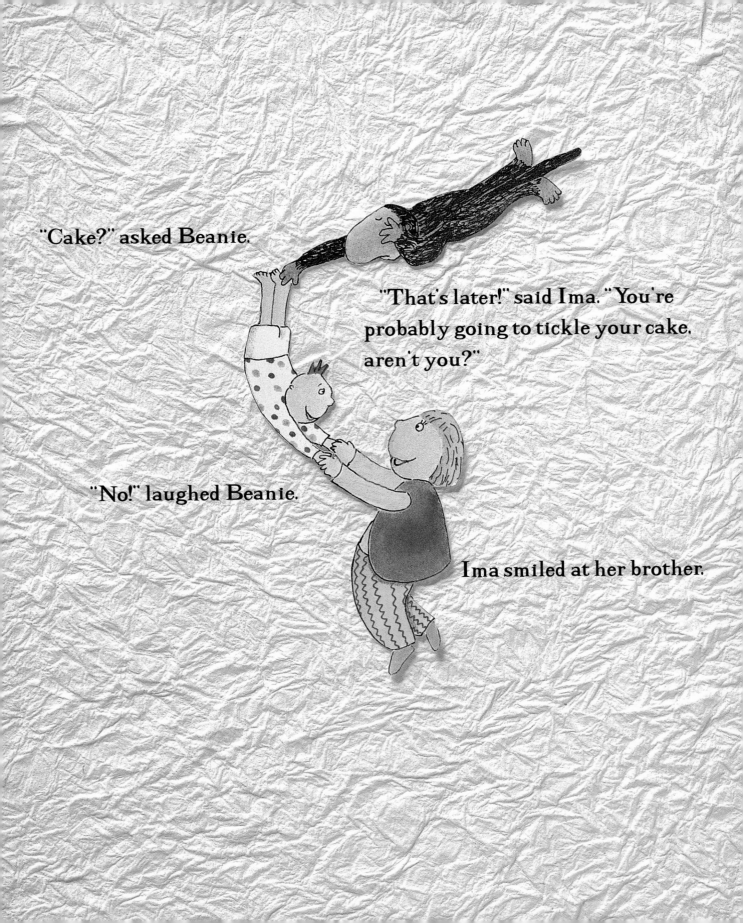

"Cake?" asked Beanie.

"That's later!" said Ima. "You're probably going to tickle your cake, aren't you?"

"No!" laughed Beanie.

Ima smiled at her brother.

After breakfast, Ima and Jake left to pick up the cake.

In all the commotion, nobody noticed that Beanie and Harry had gone along, too.

The baker brought out Beanie's cake.
"It's *beautiful!*" said Ima. "Those wings
make the cake look like it could fly!"

"Let's see!" said Jake as he swooped up the cake and threw it.

Beanie tried to go after his cake,
but Harry held him tight.
Ima ran to catch the cake, but it
landed on the roof of a passing car.
"Now you've done it!" shouted Ima.
"Follow that cake!"

"My caaaake!" cried Beanie.

"Beanie?" said Ima. "You can't wait to get your cake, can you?"

Meanwhile, Mr. and Mrs. Garbanzo had discovered that Beanie and Harry were missing. "They must have followed Jake and Ima to the bakery.

Let's go

ooooooooooo get them!",

said Mrs. Garbanzo.

As Mr. and Mrs. Garbanzo flew overhead, the driver in the car with the cake on top stopped to watch.

Ima reached for the cake.

"Beanie! Harry!"

"What are you doing?" asked Mrs. Garbanzo.

"Trying to get the cake," said Ima.

"My caaaaaaake!"

shouted Beanie.

The Garbanzos got
home just before the
guests arrived.

At the party, they performed
one of their World-Famous
Flying Garbanzo family flips.
All Beanie wanted was his cake.
Josephine held the cake up high until
it was time to sing "Happy Birthday."

"Now you can have your cake!" said Mr. Garbanzo.

"Let me see . . ." said Mrs. Garbanzo. "I know you're not going to hug your cake!"

"You said you wouldn't tickle your cake," said Ima.

"And you're definitely *not* going to kiss your cake!" said Jake.

"I bet you're going to eat your cake!" said Mr. Garbanzo.

"No," said Beanie as he blew out the candles . . .

and jumped . . .

...into the cake!

"Yummo!"